Hugh McHugh

Back To the Woods

Hugh McHugh

Back To the Woods

1st Edition | ISBN: 978-3-75236-089-9

Place of Publication: Frankfurt am Main, Germany

Year of Publication: 2020

Outlook Verlag GmbH, Germany.

BACK TO THE WOODS

The Story of a Fall from Grace

BY HUGH McHUGH

CHAPTER I.

Seven, come eleven!

After promising Clara J. that I would never again light a pipe at the race track, there I stood, one of the busiest puff-puff laddies on the circuit.

Well, the truth of the matter is just this: I fell asleep at the switch and somebody put the white lights all over me.

Just how I happened to join the Dream Builders' Association I don't know, but for several weeks I was Willie the Wild Boy at the race track and I kept all the Bookmakers busy trying not to laugh when they took my money.

Every day when I showed up at the gate the Pipers played "Darling, Dream of Me!" and every time I picked a skate the Smokers' Society went into executive session and elected me a life member.

Every horse that finished last gave me the trembling lip as he crawled home, well aware of the fact that I had caught him with the goods.

I blame Bunch Jefferson for putting the bug in my Central.

Bunch went down to the skating pond one day with $18 and picked four live wires at an average of 8 to 1. Then he began to talk about himself.

After that event whenever I happened to meet Bunch he would raise his megaphone and fill the neighborhood with hot ozone, fresh from the oven.

It was pitiful to see that boy swell.

Just to cure Bunch and drive him out of the balloon business I made up my mind one day I'd run down to the Flatfish Factory and drag a few honest dollars away from the Bookmakers.

Splash!

That's where I fell overboard.

One bright Saturday P. M. found me clinging to a wad the size of a fountain pen and trying to decide whether I'd better play Dinkalorum at 40 to 1 or Hysterics at 9 to 5.

I finally decided that a ten-spot on Dinkalorum would net me enough to give Bunch a line of sad talk, so I stepped up to the poor-box and contributed.

Dinkalorum started off in the lead like a pale streak and I immediately bought an entirely new set of furniture for the flat.

About half way around a locomotive whistle happened to blow near by. Dinkalorum, being a Union horse, thought it was six o'clock and refused absolutely to work a minute overtime.

I had to put the furniture back in the store.

In the next race I decided to play a system of my own invention so I took my program, counted seven up, four down and two up, all of which resulted in Pink Slob at 60 to 1.

It looked good and I handed Isadore Longfinger $10 for the purpose of tearing $600 away from him a little later on.

Pink Slob got away in the lead but he made the mistake of walking fast instead of running, with the result that when the other horses were back in the stable Pinkie was still giving a heel and toe exhibition around near third base.

It wasn't my day, so I squeezed into the thirst parlor and bathed my injured feelings with sarsaparilla.

Just before the last race I ran across Bunch. He was over $300 to the good and he wanted to treat me to a lot of kind words he felt like saying about himself.

Oh! but maybe he wasn't the City Boy with the Head in the Suburbs!

When I reached home that night I felt like a sock that needs darning.

Clara J. had invited Uncle Peter to take dinner with us and he began to give me the nervous look-over as soon as I answered roll call.

Uncle Peter is a very stout, old gentleman. When he squeezes into our little flat the walls act like they are bow-legged.

Uncle Peter always goes through the folding doors sideways and every time he sits down the man in the flat below kicks because we move the piano so often.

Tacks was also present.

Tacks is my youthful brother-in-law with a mind like a walking delegate because he's always looking for trouble and when he finds it he passes it up to somebody who doesn't need it.

"Evening, John!" gurgled Uncle Peter; "late, aren't you?"

"Cars blocked, delayed me," I sighed.

"New York will be a nice place when they get it finished, won't it?" chirped Tacks.

Just then Aunt Martha squeezed in from a shopping excursion and I went out in the hall while she counted up and dragged out the day's spoils for Clara J. to look at.

Aunt Martha is Uncle Peter's wife only she weighs more and breathes oftener.

When the two of them visit our bird cage at the same time the janitor has to go out and stand in front of the building with a view to catching it if it falls.

That night I waded into all the sporting papers and burned dream pipes till the smoke made me dizzy.

The next day I hit the track with three sure-fires and a couple of perhapses.

There was nothing to it. All I had to do was to keep my nerve and not get side-tracked and I'd have enough coin to make Andrew Carnegie's check book look like a punched meal ticket.

I played them—and when the Angelus was ringing Moses O'Brien and three other Bookbinders were out buying meal tickets with my money.

Things went along this way for about a week and I was all to the bad.

One evening Clara J. said to me, "John, I looked through your check book to-day and I've had a cold on my chest ever since. At first I thought I had opened the refrigerator by mistake."

At last the blow had fallen!

I had promised her faithfully before we were married that I'd never play the ponies again and I fell and broke my word.

The accident was painful, and I'd be a sad scamp to put her wise at this late day, especially after being fried to a finish.

I simply didn't dare confess that my money had gone into a fund to furnish a home for Incurable Bookmakers—what to do? What to do?

She had me lashed to the mast.

4

"May I inquire," my wife continued with the breath of winter in her tones, "why it's all going out and nothing coming in? Have you begun so soon to lead a double life?"

Mother, call your baby boy back home! If Uncle Peter would only drop in, or Tacks or Aunt Martha or even the janitor!

Suddenly it occurred to me:

"Dearie," I said, "you have surprised my secret, and now nothing remains but the pleasure of telling you everything."

A thaw set in.

"As you have stated, not incorrectly, my dear, large bundles of Green Fellows have severed their home ties and tiptoed into the elsewhere," I continued, gradually getting my nerve back.

The thermometer continued to go up.

"Clara J., on several occasions you have expressed a desire to leave this torn-up city and retire to the woodlands, haven't you?" I asked.

She nodded and the weather grew warmer.

"Once you said to me, 'Oh, John, if they'd only take New York off the operating table and give the poor city a chance to get well, how nice it would be!'—didn't you?"

Another nod.

"Well," I said, backing Munchausen in a corner and dragging his medals away from him, "that's the answer, You for the Burbs! You for the chateau up the track! Henceforth, you for the cage in the country where the daffydowndillys sing in the treetops and buttercups chirp from bough to bough!"

"Oh, John!" she exclaimed, faint with delight; "do you really mean you've bought a home in the country? How perfectly lovely! You, dear, dear, old John! And that's what you've been doing with all your money, just to surprise me! Bless your dear good heart! Oh! I'm so glad, and so delighted. Won't it be simply grand?"

I could feel the cold, spectral form of Sapphira leaning over my left shoulder, urging me on.

"What is it like? How many rooms? Where is it?" she inquired, all in one breath.

Where was the blamed thing? What did it look like? How did I know? She could search me. I could feel my ears getting red. Presently I braced and

5

mumbled, "No more details till the castle is completed, then I'll coax you out there and let you revel."

"How soon will that be?" she asked, "To-morrow? Yes, John, to-morrow?"

"No," I whispered croupily, "in—in about a week."

I wanted time to arrange my earthly affairs.

"Oh! lovely!" she said, and kissing me rushed away to break the news to mother.

I felt like a rain check after the sun comes out.

Suddenly Hope tugged at my heart strings and I remembered that I had a week in which to beat the ponies to a pulp and win out enough coin to buy six Swiss Cheese cottages in the country.

Day after day I waded in among the jelly fish at the track but the best I ever got was an $8 win.

Eight dollars wouldn't buy a dog house.

I was desperate. Every evening I had to sit around and listen while Clara J. told Tacks or Uncle Peter or Aunt Martha or Mother what she intended doing when we moved to the country.

They had it all cooked up. Uncle Peter and Aunt Martha were coming to live with us and Tacks would be there to let us live with him.

Uncle Peter intended starting a garden truck farm in the back yard and Tacks figured on building a chicken coop somewhere between the front gate and the parlor.

Aunt Martha and Clara J. almost came to blows over the question of milking the cow. Aunt Martha insisted that cows are milked by machinery and Clara J. was equally positive that moral suasion is the only means by which a cow can be brought to a show down.

In the meantime I was dying every half hour.

Finally the day preceding the long-talked of country excursion arrived and I began to figure on the safest and least inexpensive methods of suicide.

I went to the track in the afternoon and threw out enough gold dust to paint our country home from cellar to attic—but never a sardine showed.

Frostbitten and suffocated by the odor of burning money I crept into a seat in the car and began to plan my finale.

Presently an elbow poked me in the ribs and I looked into the smiling face of

Bunch Jefferson.

"Still piking, eh?" he chuckled; "you wouldn't trail along after Your Uncle Bunch and get next to the candy man, would you? Only $400 to the good to-day. Am I the picker from Picklesburg, son of the old man Pickwick?—well, I guess yes!"

Then in that desperate moment I broke down and confessed all to Bunch. I told him how my haughty spirit disdained a tip and how in the pride of my heart I doped the cards myself and fell in the well. I told him of my feverish desire to beat the Bookmakers down through the earth till they yelled for mercy, and I told him of my pitiful dilemma and how I had to build a home in the country before noon to-morrow or do a dog trot to the Bad lands.

Then Bunch began to laugh—a long, loud, discordant laugh which ended in, "John, I'll help you make good!" and then I began to sit up and notice things.

"I'm away head of this pitty-pat game at the Merry-go-Round," Bunch went on, "and it so happens that recently I peeled the wrapper off my roll and swapped it for a country home for my sister and her daughter. She's a young widow, my sister is, and one of the loveliest little ladies that ever came over the hill. And she has a daughter that's a regular plate of peaches and cream."

Still I sat in darkness, and he went on:

"Now, my sister won't move out there for a day or two, so to-morrow, promptly on schedule time, you lead your domestic fleet over the sandbars to that house and point with pride to its various beauties—are you wise?"

"But, Great Scott, man! it's not mine!" I gasped.

"Roll a small pill and get together," admonished Bunch, with a seraphic smile. "Can't you figure the trick to win? All you have to do is to coax your gang out there and then break the painful news to them that you've suddenly discovered the place is haunted and that you're going to sell it and buy a better bandbox—getting wise?"

"Bunch," I murmured, weakly, "you've saved my life, temporarily, at least. Where is this palace?"

"Only forty minutes from the City Hall—any old City Hall," he answered, "It's at Jiggersville, on the Sitfast & Chewsmoke R.R., eighteen miles from Anywhere, hot and cold sidewalks and no mosquitoes in the winter. Here you are, full particulars," and with this Bunch handed me a printed card which let me into all the secrets of that haven of rest in the tall grass.

Bless good old Bunch!

I offered to buy him a quart of Ruinart but he said his thirst wasn't working,

7

so I had to paddle off home.

That evening for the first time in several weeks I felt like speaking to myself.

I was the life of the party and I even beamed approvingly when Uncle Peter tuned up his mezzo contralto voice and began to write a book about the delights of a country home.

It was a cinch, I assured myself, that the ghost story I had broiled up to tell on the morrow would send my suburban-mad family scurrying back to town.

Many times mentally I went over the blood curdling details and I flattered myself that I surely had a lot of shivery goods for sale.

I couldn't see myself losing at all, at all.

So me for Jiggersville in the morning.

CHAPTER II.

When the alarm clock went to work the next morning Clara J. turned around and gave it a look that made its teeth chatter.

She had been up and doing an hour before that clock grew nervous enough to crow.

Her enthusiasm was so great that she was a Busy-Lizzie long before 7 o'clock and we were not booked to leave the Choo-Choo House till 10:30.

About 8 o'clock she dragged me away from a dream and I reluctantly awoke to a realization of the fact that I was due to deliver some goods which I had never seen and didn't want to see.

"Get up, John!" Clara J. suggested, with a degree of excitement in her voice; "it's getting dreadfully late and you know I'm all impatience to see that lovely home you've bought for me in the country!"

[Illustration: Clara J.—A Dream of Peaches—Please Pass the Cream.]

Me under the covers, gnawing holes in the pillow to keep from swearing.

"Oh, dear me!" she sighed, "I'm afraid I'm just a bit sorry to leave this sweet little apartment. We've been so happy here, haven't we?"

I grabbed the ball and broke through the center for 10 yards.

"Sorry," I echoed, tearfully; "why, it's breaking my heart to leave this cozy little collar box of a home and go into a great large country house full of—of —of rooms, and—er—and windows, and—er—and—er—piazzas, and—and —and cows and things like that."

"Of course we wouldn't have to keep the cow in the house," she said, thoughtfully.

"Oh, no," I said, "that's the point. There would be a barn, and you haven't any idea how dangerous barns are. They are the curse of country life, barns are."

"Well, then, John, why did you buy the cow?" she inquired, and I went up and punched a hole in the plaster.

Why did I buy the cow? Was there a cow? Had Bunch ever mentioned a cow to me? Come to think of it he hadn't and there I was cooking trouble over a slow fire.

When I came to she was saying quietly, "Besides, I think I'd rather have a milkman than a cow. Milkmen swear a lot and cheat sometimes but as a rule they are more trustworthy than cows, and they very seldom chase anybody. Couldn't you turn the barn into a gymnasium or something?"

"Dearie," I said, trying my level best to get a mist over my lamps so as to give her the teardrop gaze, "something keeps whispering to me, 'Sidestep that cave in the wilderness!' Something keeps telling me that a month on the farm will put a crimp in our happiness, and that the moment we move into a home in the tall grass ill luck will get up and put the boots to our wedded bliss."

Then I gave an imitation of a choking sob which sounded for all the world like the last dying shriek of a bathtub when the water is busy leaving it.

"Nonsense, John!" laughed Clara J.; "it's only natural that you regret leaving our first home, but after one day in the country you'll be happy as a king."

"Make it a deuce," I muttered; "a dirty deuce at that."

"Now," she said, joyfully; "I'm going to cook your breakfast. This may be your very last breakfast in a city apartment for months, maybe years, so I'm going to cook it myself. I've got every trunk packed—haven't I worked hard? Get up, you lazy boy!" and with this she danced out of the room.

Every trunk packed! Did she intend taking them with her, and if she did how could I stop her?

Back to the woods!

I began to feel like a street just before they put the asphalt down.

For some time I lay there with my brain huddled up in one corner of my head, fluttering and frightened.

Presently an insistent scratch-r-r-r aroused me and I began to sit up and notice things.

The things I noticed consisted chiefly of Tacks and the kitchen carving knife. The former was seated on the floor laboriously engineering the latter in an endeavor to produce a large arrow-pierced heart on the polished panel of the bedroom door.

"What's the idea?" I inquired.

"I'm farewelling the place," he answered, mournfully. "They's only two more doors to farewell after I get this one finished. Ain't hearts awful hard to drawr just right, 'specially when the knife slips!"

"You little imp!" I yelled; "do you mean to tell me you've been doing a Swinnerton all over this man's house? S'cat!" and I reached for a shoe.

"Cut it!" cried Tacks, indignantly. "Didn't the janitor say he'd miss me dreadful, and how can he miss me 'less'n he sees my loving rememberments all over the place every time he shows this compartment to somebody else? And it is impolite to go 'way forever and ever amen without farewelling the janitor!"

"Where do you think you're going?" I inquired, trying hard to be calm.

"To the country to live, sister told me," Tacks bubbled; "and we ain't never coming back to this horrid city, sister told me; and you bought the house for a surprise, sister told me; and it has a pizzazus all around it, sister told me; and a cow that gives condensed milk, sister told me; and they's hens and chickens and turkey goblins and a garden to plant potato salad, and they's a barn with pigeons in the attic, and they's a lawn with a barbers wire fence all around it, sister told me; and our trunks are all packed, and we ain't never coming back here no more, sister told me; and I must hurry and farewell them two doors!"

Tacks was slightly in the lead when my shoe reached the door, so he won.

At breakfast we were joined by Uncle Peter and Aunt Martha, both of whom fairly oozed enthusiasm and Clara J.'s pulse began to climb with excitement and anticipation.

I was on the bargain counter, marked down from 30 cents.

Every time Uncle Peter sprang a new idea in reference to his garden, and they came so fast they almost choked him, I felt a burning bead of perspiration start out to explore my forehead.

Presently to put the froth of fear upon my cup of sorrow there came a telegram from "Bunch" which read as follows:

New York ——

John Henry
No. 301 W. 109th St.

Sister and family will move in country house tomorrow be sure to play your game to-day good luck.

Bunch.

"Poor John! you look so worried," said Clara J., anxiously; "I really hope it is nothing that will call you back to town for a week at least. It will take us fully a week to get settled, don't you think so, Aunt Martha?"

I dove into my coffee cup and stayed under a long time. When I came to the

11

surface again Uncle Peter was explaining to Tacks that baked beans grew only in a very hot climate, and in the general confusion the telegram was forgotten by all except my harpooned self.

Clara J. and Aunt Martha were both tearful when we left the flat to ride to the station, but to my intense relief no mention was made of the trunks, consequently I began to lift the mortgage from my life and breathe easier.

On the way out Tacks left a small parcel with one of the hall boys with instructions to hand it to the janitor as soon as possible.

"It's a little present for the janitor in loving remembrance of his memory," Tacks explained with something that sounded like a catch in his voice.

"Hasn't that boy a lovely disposition?" Aunt Martha beamed on Tacks; "to be so forgiving to the janitor after the horrid man had sworn at him and blamed him for putting a cat in the dumb waiter and sending it up to the nervous lady on the seventh floor who abominated cats and who screamed and fell over in a tub of suds when she opened the dumb-waiter door to get her groceries and the cat jumped at her. Mercy! how can the boy be so generous!"

Tacks bore up bravely under this panegyric of praise and his face wore a rapt expression which amounted almost to religious fervor.

"What did you give the janitor, Angel-Face?" I asked.

"Only just another remembrance," Tacks answered, solemnly. "I happened to find a poor, little dead mouse under the gas range and I thought I'd farewell the janitor with it."

Aunt Martha sighed painfully and Uncle Peter chuckled inwardly like a mechanical toy hen.

On the train out to Jiggersville Clara J. was a picture entitled, "The Joy of Living"—kind regards to Mrs. Pat Campbell; Ibsen please write.

As for me with every revolution of the wheels I grew more and more like a half portion of chipped beef.

"Oh, John!" said Clara J., her voice shrill with excitement; "I forgot to tell you! I left my key with Mother, and she's going to superintend the packing of the furniture this afternoon. By evening she expects to have everything loaded in the van and we won't have to wait any time for our trunks and things!"

"Great Scott!" I yelled; "maybe you won't like the house! Maybe it's only a shanty with holes in the roof—er, I mean, maybe you'll be disappointed with the lay-out! What's the blithering sense of being in such a consuming fever about moving the fiendish furniture? I'm certain you'll hate the very sight of this corn-crib out among the ant hills. Can't you back-pedal on the furniture gag and give yourself a chance to hear the answer to what you ask yourself?"

Clara J. looked tearfully at me for a moment; then she went over and sat with Aunt Martha and told her how glad she was we were moving to the country where the pure air would no doubt have a soothing effect on my nerves because I certainly had grown irritable of late.

At last we reached the little old log cabin down the lane and after the first glimpse I knew it was all off.

The place I had borrowed from Bunch for a few minutes was a dream, all right, all right.

With its beautiful lawns and its glistening gravelled walks; with a modern house perfect in every detail; with its murmuring brooklet rushing away into a perspective of nodding green trees and with the bright sunshine smiling a welcome over all it made a picture calculated to charm the most hardened city crab that ever crawled away from the cover of the skyscrapers.

As for Clara J. she simply threw up both hands and screamed for help. She danced and yelled with delight. Then she hugged and kissed me with a thousand reiterated thanks for my glorious present.

I felt as joyous as a jelly fish. Ten-legged microbes began to climb into my pores. Everything I had in my system rushed to my head. I could see myself in the giggle-giggle ward in a bat house, playing I was the king of England.

I was a joke turned upside down.

After they had examined every nook and cranny of the place and had talked themselves hoarse with delight I called them all up on the front piazza for the purpose of putting out their lights with my ghost story.

I figured on driving them all back to the depot with about four paragraphs of creepy talk, so when I had them huddled I began in a hoarse whisper to raise their hair.

I told them that no doubt they had noticed the worried expression on my face and explained that it was due chiefly to the fact that I had learned quite by accident that this beautiful place was haunted.

Tacks grew so excited that he dropped a garden spade off the piazza and into a hot house below, breaking seven panes of glass, but the others only smiled indulgently and I went on.

I jumped head first into my most blood-curdling story and related in detail how a murder had been committed on the very site the house was built on and how a fierce bewhiskered spirit roamed the premises at night and demanded vengeance. I described in awful words the harrowing spectacle and all I got at

13

the finish was the hoot from Uncle Peter.

"Poor John," said Clara J., "I had no idea you were so run down. Why, you're almost on the verge of nervous prostration. And how thoughtful you were to pick out a haunted house, for I do love ghosts. Didn't you know that? I'll tell you what let's do. I'll give a prize for the first one who sees and speaks to this unhappy spirit—won't it be jolly? Where are you going, John?"

"Me, to the undertakers—I mean I must run back to town. That telegram this morning—important business—forgot all about it—see you later—don't breathe till I get back—I mean, don't live till I—Oh! the devil!"

Just then I fell over the lawn mower, picked myself up hastily and rushed off to town to find Bunch for I was certainly up against it good and hard.

CHAPTER III.

When finally I located Bunch and told him the bitter truth he acted like a zee-zee boy in a Wheel House.

Laugh! Say! he just threw out his chest and cackled a solo that fairly bit its way through my anatomy.

Every once in a white he'd give me the red-faced glare and snicker, "Oh, you mark! You Cincherine! You to the seltzer bottle—fizz!—fizz! The only and original Wheeze Puller, not! You're all right—backwards!"

Then he'd throw his ears back and let a chortle out of his thirst-teaser that made the neighborhood jump sideways and rubber for a cop.

"What are you going to do?" he asked me when presently his face grew too tired to hold any more wrinkles.

[Illustration: Uncle Peter—the Original Trust Tamer.]

"Give me the count," I sighed; 'I'm down and out."

"Have you no plan at all?" inquired Bunch.

"Plan, nothing," I said; "every time I try to think of a plan my brain gets bashful and hides. There's nothing in my noddle now but a headache."

"Well," said Bunch, "I'll throw a wire at my sister and tell her not to move out to Jiggersville until day after to-morrow. In the mean time we'll have to get a crowbar and pry your family circle loose from my premises. Nothing doing in the ghost business, eh?"

"Nothing," I answered, mournfully; "I couldn't coax a shiver."

"A fire wouldn't do, would it?" Bunch suggested, thoughtfully.

"It wouldn't do for you, unless you are aces with the insurance Indians," I answered.

"We-o-o-u-w!" yelled Bunch, "I have it—burglars!"

"Burglars!" I repeated, mechanically.

"Sure! it's a pipe!" Bunch went on with enthusiasm. "You will play Spike Hennessy and I'll be Gumshoe Charlie. We'll disguise ourselves with whiskers and break into the house about 2 o'clock in the morning. We'll arouse the sleeping inmates, shoot our bullet-holders in the ceiling once or

15

twice and hand them enough excitement to make them gallop back to town on the first train. Do you follow me, eh, what?"

"Not me, Bunch," I shook my head sadly. "Nix on the burgle for yours truly. I must take the next train back to the woods. Otherwise wee wifey may suspect something and begin to pass me out the zero language. But I like the burglar idea. Couldn't you do it as a monologue?"

"What! all by my lonesome?" cried Bunch. "Say! John, doesn't that sound like making me work a trifle too hard to get my own goods back ?"

I sighed and looked as helpless as a nut under the hammer.

Bunch laughed again. "Oh, very well," he said, "I see I'm the only life-saver on duty so I'll do a single specialty and pull you out of the pickle bottle."

I grasped my rescuer's hand and shook it warmly in silence.

"Leave a front window open," Bunch directed, "and somewhere around two o'clock I'll squeeze through."

"I'll have it worked up good and proper," I said, eagerly. "I'll throw out dark hints all the evening and have the bunch ready to quiver when the crash comes. As soon as I hear your signal I'll rush bravely down stairs and you shoot the ceiling. I'll give you a struggle and chase you outside. Then I'll run you down behind the barn. There, free from observation, you can shoot a couple of holes in my coat so that I can produce evidence of a fierce fight, and then you to the tall timber. I'll crawl breathlessly back to my palpitating household, and, displaying my wounded coat, declare everything off. I'll refuse to live any longer in a house where murder and sudden death occupy the spare room. It looks to me like a cinchalorum, Bunch, a regular cinchalorum!"

"It sounds good," Bunch acquiesced, "and I'll give you an imitation of the best little amateur cracksman that ever swung a jimmy. I'll take a late train out and hang around till it's time to ring the curtain up. By the way, are there any revolvers on the premises?"

"Not a gun," I answered, "not even an ice-pick. Uncle Peter won't show fight. All he'll show will be a blonde night gown cutting across lots to beat the breeze. Aunt Martha will climb to the attic, Clara J. will be busy doing a scream solo, and Tacks will crawl under the bed and pull the bed after him. There'll be no interference, Bunch; it's easy money!"

With this complete understanding we parted and I hustled back to Jiggersville.

I found the family still delirious with delight with the exception of Clara J.

whose enthusiasm had been dampened by my sudden departure.

My reappearance brought her back to earth, however, and in the presence of so many new excitements she didn't even question me with regard to my City trip.

As the evening wore on my nervousness increased and I began to wonder if Bunch would really turn the trick or give me the loud snicker and leave me flat.

I had gone too far now to confess everything to Clara J. She'd never forgive me.

If I told her the facts in the case the long Arctic Winter Night would set in, and I'd be playing an icicle on the window frame.

I felt as lonely as a coal scuttle during the strike.

About six o'clock Uncle Peter waded into the sitting room, flushed and happy as a school boy. "I've just left the garden," he chuckled.

"No, you haven't," I said, glancing at his shoes; "you've brought most of it in here with you."

I never touched him. The old gentleman sat down in a loud rocker and began to tell me a lot of things I didn't want to hear. Uncle Peter always intersperses his remarks on current topics with bits of parboiled philosophy that make one want to get up and drive him through the carpet with a tack hammer. When it comes to wise saws and proverbial stunts Uncle Peter has Solomon backed up in the corner.

"John," he said, "this country life is great. Early to bed and early to rise makes a man's stomach digest mince pies—how's that? Notice the air out here? How pure and fresh and bracing! You ought to go out and run a mile, John!"

"I'd like to run ten miles," I answered, truthfully.

"Exercise, that's the essence of life, my boy!" he continued. "I firmly believe I could run five miles to-day without straining a muscle."

I laughed internally and thought of the glorious opportunity he'd have before the morning broke.

"You may or may not know, John," the old gentleman kept on, "that I was a remarkably fine swordsman in my younger days. Parry, thrust, cut, slash— heigho! those were the times. And, to tell you the truth, I'm still able to hold my own with the sword or pistol. I found a sword hanging on the wall in the hall to-day and I've been practising a few swings."

17

A vision of Uncle Peter running a rusty sword into the interior department of the disguised and disgusted Bunch rose before me, but I blew it away with a laugh.

"He laughs best who laughs in his sleeve," chuckled the old party. "Now that we're out in the country all of us should learn to handle a sword or a pistol. It gives us self reliance. It's very different from living in the city, I tell you. A tramp in the lock-up is worth two in the kitchen. I shot at a mark for an hour to-day."

"What with?" I gasped.

"With a bow and arrow I bought for Tacks yesterday directly I learned we were coming to the country. I hit the bull's eye five out of six times. An ounce of prevention is worth two hundred pounds of policemen, you know. Tacks practised, too, and drove an arrow through a strange man's overalls and was chased half a mile for his skill in marksmanship, but, as I said before, the exercise will do him good."

"Where do you keep this bow and arrow?" I inquired, with a studied assumption of carelessness.

"To-night I'll keep it under my pillow. *Honi soit qui oncle Pierre*, which means, evil be to him who monkeys with Uncle Peter," he said, solemnly. "To-morrow I'm going to town to buy a bull dog revolver, maybe a bull dog *and* a revolver, for a dog in the manger is the noblest Roman of them all."

I could see poor Bunch scooting across the lawn with a bunch of arrows in his ramparts and Uncle Peter behind, prodding his citadel with a carving knife.

I began to get a hunch that our plan of campaign was threatened with an attack of busy Uncle Peter, and I had just about decided to remove his door key and lock the old man up in his room when Clara J. came in to announce dinner.

Aunt Martha and Clara J. had collaborated on the dinner and it was a success. Uncle Peter said so, and his appetite is one of those brave fighting machines that never says die till every plate is clean.

I was so nervous I couldn't eat a bite, but I pleaded a toothache, so they all gave me the sympathetic stare and passed me up.

We went to bed early and I rehearsed mentally the stage business for the drama about to be enacted when Bunch crept through the picket lines.

About midnight a dog in the neighborhood began to hurl forth a series of the most distressing bow-bows I ever heard. I arose, put up the window and looked out.

I saw a tall man with a bunch of whiskers on his face flying across the lot pursued by a black-and-tan pup, which snapped eagerly at the man's heels and seemed determined to eat him up if ever the runner stopped long enough.

I felt in my bones that the one in the lead was Bunch, and I sighed deeply and went back to bed.

I must have dropped into an uneasy sleep for Clara J. was tapping me on the arm when I started up and asked the answer.

"There's somebody in the house," she whispered, not a bit frightened, to my surprise and dismay, "Maybe it's only the ghost you told us about—what a lark!"

"Somebody in the house," I muttered, going on the stage blindly to play my part; "and there isn't a gun in the castle."

"Yes there is," she answered, joyfully, I fancied; "mother brought father's revolver over yesterday and made me put it in my satchel. She said we would feel safer at night with it in the house. Do let me shoot him; I can aim straight, indeed I can! Why, John, what makes you tremble so?"

"I'm not trembling, you goose!" I snarled; "I can't find my shoes, that's all. Doggone if I'm going to live in a joint like this with ghosts and burglars all over the place."

Just then an alarming yell ascended from the regions below, followed by a crash and a series of the most picturesque, sulphur-lined oaths that mortal man ever gave vent to.

It was Bunch. His trademark was on every word. I could recognize his brimstone vocabulary with my eyes shut.

But what dire fate had befallen him? Surely, not even an amateur cracksman would give himself and the whole snap away unless the provocation was great.

Lights began to appear all over the house. Aunt Martha in a weird makeup came out of her room screaming, "What is it? What is it?" followed by Uncle Peter and his trusty bow and arrow.

I began to pray. It was all over. A rosewood casket for Bunch.
Me for the Morgue.

Just as I was ready to rush down to investigate, Tacks came bounding up the stairs, two steps at a time, clad only in his nightie.

Up the stairs, mind you! The nerve of that kid!

"Gi'me the prize, sister!" he yelled; "I caught the ghost! I caught him!"

"What do you mean?" I said, shaking him.

Tacks grinned from ear to ear. "You know they's a trap door in the hall so's to get down in the cellar and it ain't finished yet, so this evening I took the door up and laid heavy paper on it so's if the ghost walked on it he'd go through and he did, and I get the prize, don't I, sister?"

I rushed down to the scene of the explosion, followed by my excited household.

Leaning over the yawning cellar trap door I yelled, "Who's down there?"

"Oh! you go to hell!" came back the voice of the disgusted Bunch, whereupon Aunt Martha almost fainted, while Uncle Peter loaded his bow and arrow and prepared to sell his life dearly.

Great Scott! what a situation! The man who owned the house nursing his bruises in the muddy cellar while the bunch of interlopers above him clamored for his life.

While I puzzled my dizzy think-factory for a way out of the dilemma there came a terrific knock at the door and Tacks promptly opened it.

"Have you got him? Have you got him?" inquired the elongated and cadaverous specimen of humanity who burst into the hall and stared at us.

"I seen him early this evening a'hangin' around these here premises and I ups and chases him twicet, but the skunk outrun me," the newcomer gurgled, as he excitedly swung a policeman's billy the size of a fence rail.

"Then I seen the lights here and says I, 'they has him'! Perduce the maleyfactor till I trot him to the lock-up!" and with this the minion of the law rolled up his sleeves and prepared for action.

"I presume you are the chief of police?" inquired Uncle Peter, with an affable smile.

"I'm all the police they is and my name is Harmony Diggs, and they's no buggular livin' can get out'n my clutches oncet I gits these boys on him," the visitor shouted, waving an antiquated pair of handcuffs excitedly in the air.

Tacks watched him open-mouthed. That boy was having the time of his life and it would have pleased me immeasurably to paddle him to sleep with Harmony's night stick.

"I caught him!" Tacks cried in exultant tones when the village copper looked his way; "he's down there."

"Down there, eh?" snorted the country Sherlock, getting on his knees and peering into the depths, but just then Bunch handed him a handful of hard mud which located temporarily over Harmony's left eye and put his optic on the blink.

With the other eye, however, Mr. Diggs caught a glimpse of a step ladder, which he immediately lowered through the trap, and drawing a murderous looking revolver from his pocket, commanded Bunch to come up or be shot.

Bunch decided to come up. I didn't hold the watch on him, but I figure it took him about seven-sixteenths of a second to make the decision.

As the criminal slowly emerged from the cellar the spectators stood back, spellbound and breathless; Aunt Martha with a long tin dipper raised in an attitude of defense, and Uncle Peter with the bow and arrow ready for instant use.

These war-like precautions were unnecessary, however. Bunch was a sight. His clothing had accumulated all the mud in the unfinished cellar and his false whiskers were skewed around, giving his face the expression of a prize gorilla.

Bunch looked at me reproachfully, but never opened his head. Say! if ever there was a dead game sport, Bunch Jefferson is the answer.

He didn't even whimper when the village Hawkshaw snapped the bracelets on his wrist and said, "Come on, Mr. Buggular! This here's a fine night's work for everybody in this neighborhood because you've been a source of pesterment around here for six months. If you don't get ten years, Mr. Buggular, then I ain't no guess maker. Come along; goodnight to you, one and all; that there boy that catched this buggular ought to get rewarded nice!"

"He will be," I said mentally, as Mr. Diggs led the suffering Bunch away to the Bastile.

"I've got to see that villain landed in a cell," I said to Clara J. as the door closed on the victor and vanquished.

"Do, John!" she answered; "but don't be too hard on the poor fellow. You can't tell what temptations may have led him astray. I certainly am disappointed for I was sure it was the ghost. Anyway, the burglar had whiskers like the ghost's, didn't he?"

I didn't stop to reply, but grabbing my coat rushed away to formulate some plan to get Bunch out of hock.

CHAPTER IV.

JOHN HENRY'S COUNTRY COP.

Ahead of me, plodding along the pike under the moonlight, were Bunch and his cadaverous captor, the former bowed in sorrow or anger, probably both, and the latter with head erect, haughty as a Roman conqueror.

Bunch's make-up was a troubled dream. Over a pair of hand-me-down trousers, eight sizes too large for him, he wore a three-dollar ulster. On his head was an automobile cap, and his face was covered with a bunch of eelgrass three feet deep. He was surely all the money.

As I drew near I could hear Mr. Diggs expatiating on crime in general and housebreaking in particular, and I fancied I could also hear Bunch boiling and seething within.

[Illustration: Aunt Martha—a Short, Stout Bundle of Good Nature.]

"Mr. Buggular," Diggs was saying, "I don't know just what your home trainin' was as a child, but they's a screw loose somewhere or you'd a'never been brought to this here harrowful perdickyment, nohow. I s'pose you jest started in nat'rally to be a heenyus maleyfactor early in life, huh? You needn't to answer if you're afeared it'll incrimigate you, but I s'pose you took to it when a boy, pickin' pockets or suthin' like that, huh?"

"Oh, cut it out, you old goat, and don't bother me!" snapped Bunch, just as I joined them.

"A dangerous maleyfactor," said Diggs to me, as he tightened his grip on Bunch's arm; "but they ain't no call for you to assist the course of justice, because if the dern critter starts to run I'll pump him chuck full of lead. He's been a'tellin' me he started on the downward path to predition as a child-stealer."

"I told you nothing, you old tadpole," shrieked Bunch, unable to contain himself longer.

"Very well," said Harmony, soothingly, "they ain't no call for you to say nothin' more that'll incrimigate you before the bar of Justice. Steady, now, or I'll tap you with this here cane!"

"Brace up, good old sport; I'll get you out of this in a jiffy," I whispered to Bunch at the first opportunity, and he gave me a cold-storage look that chased the chills all over me.

Presently we arrived at the little brick structure which Jiggersville proudly called its calaboose, and after much fumbling of keys, Mr. Diggs opened the jackpot and we all stayed.

The yap policeman was for taking Bunch right back to the donjon cell in the rear, but with a $5 bill I secured a stay of proceedings.

My forehead was damp with perspiration so I took off my hat and laid it on the bench in the little court room where Bunch sat moodily and with bowed head.

Then I coaxed the rural Vidocq over in the corner and gave him a game of talk that I thought would warm his heart, but he listened in dumbness and couldn't see "no sense in believing the maleyfactor was anythin' more'n a derned cuss, nohow!"

"I have every reason to believe that we have made a mistake," I said to Harmony in a hoarse whisper. "From an envelope dropped by this party in my house I am lead to believe that he's a respectable gentleman who entered my premises quite by mistake."

The chin whiskers owned and engineered by Diggs bobbed up and down as he chewed a reflective cud, but he couldn't see the matter in my light at all.

I had used all kinds of arguments and was just about to give up in despair when a voice in the doorway caused us both to turn.

There stood Bunch Jefferson, the real fellow, looking as fresh as a daisy.

"What's the trouble, John?" he asked, smiling benignly on Diggs.

While I was talking to the representative of the law, Mr. Slick saw his opportunity and grabbed it by the hind leg. He had quietly reached the door, and once outside the sledding was excellent.

Bunch had his business suit on under the burglar make-up. It didn't take him two minutes to work the shine darbies over his hands. He then peeled off the ulster and the tuppeny trousers, and throwing these and the Svengalis over the fence, he was home again from the Bad Lands.

The transformation scene was made complete by the fact that Bunch was now wearing my hat.

In answer to Bunch's question, the redoubtable Diggs smiled indulgently and said with pride-choked tones, "A maleyfactor, sir, caught in the meshes of the law and hauled before this here trybune of Justice by these hands!"

The eagle eye of Diggs was now triumphantly sighted along the arm and over

23

the bony hand to where the criminal was supposed to be, but when the gaze finally rested on an empty bench the expression of pained surprise on the old man-hunter's map was calculated to make a hen cackle.

Diggs rushed over to the bench, turned it upside down, looked behind the chairs, and then, emitting a roar that rattled the rafters, he hustled back to see if by any chance the prisoner had locked himself up in a cell.

Bunch gave the old geezer the minnehaha and yelled, "Say! you with the me-ya-ya's on the chin! Did somebody give you the hot-foot and make a quick exit?"

Diggs was now in full eruption and heavy showers of Reub lava rose from his vocal organs and fell all over the place, while he thrashed around the calaboose in a frenzy of excitement.

"Maybe you're sending out a general alarm about that human meteor that passed me on the pike a few minutes ago?" Bunch suggested.

Diggs turned and eyed him in open-mouthed silence.

"A mutt with a pink ulster and one of those pancakes on his head like the drivers of the gasoline carts wear," Bunch suggested.

"It's him! it's the maleyfactor!" exclaimed Harmony, tightening his grip on the night stick; "which way did the derned cuss go?"

Bunch pointed due south-east, and with a howl of rage Diggs sprang forward and bounced down the pike like a hungry kangaroo on its way to a lunch counter.

I began to wrap up my enjoyment and send it forth in short gurgles of merriment until Bunch pressed the button and the scene was changed to Greenland's Icy Mountains.

"Funny, isn't it?" he sneered; "regular circus, with yours in haste, Bunch Jefferson, to do the grand and lofty tumbling! I'm the Patsy, oh, maybe! It was a fine play, all right, but I didn't expect you to stack the cards!"

"On the level, Bunch, believe me, it wasn't my fault," I spluttered.

"Not your fault," he snapped back; "then I suppose it was mine! I suppose I fell down the elevator shaft just to please mother, eh? Maybe you think I dropped into the excavation just to pass the time away? Have you an idea that I dove down into the earth because I wanted to get back to the mines? Wasn't your fault, indeed! Maybe you think I fell in the well simply because I wanted to give an imitation of the old oaken bucket, yes?"

I tried to tell him all about Tacks and the ghost story, but he wouldn't stand

24

for it.

"You should have been waiting for me on the stairs," he argued, unreasonably, rubbing one of the bruises in his choice collection, "Didn't you catch me early in the evening being chased from pillar to post by everything in the neighborhood that had legs long enough to run? When I tried to hide in the corner of a farm over there, a bull dog came up on rubber shoes and bit his initials on some of my personal property before I could crawl through the fence. Every time I showed up on the pike that human accident that breathes like a man and talks like a rabbit chased me eight miles there and back. The first time I tried to approach the infernal house I fell over a grindstone and signed checks in the gravel with my nose. Hereafter, when you want a burglar, pick somebody your own size. I'm going to hunt a hospital and get sewed together again."

I put on all steam and tried to square myself, but Bunch only shook his head and said I was outlawed.

"You can't run on my race track," he exclaimed as he started for the depot; "that last race was crooked and you stood in with the dope mixer."

I watched him down the hill until he disappeared in the station, then, sad at heart, I trudged back to the old homestead that had caused all my trouble.

It was now broad daylight, but nowhere within my line of vision could I get a peep of the doughty Diggs.

No doubt he was still cutting across lots trying to head off the "maleyfactor."

CHAPTER V.

When I reached the cottage I found all the members of my household dressed for the day, and lined up on the piazza, eager for news from the battlefield.

"Gee whiz!" exclaimed Uncle Peter, "the boy is bareheaded! Where's your hat, John?"

"Mercy! I hope you're not scalped!" Aunt Martha cried, sympathetically.

I explained that the desperado put up a stiff fight against Diggs and myself and, warming up to the subject, I went into the details of a hand to hand struggle that made them all shiver and blink their lanterns.

When finally I finished with the statement that the robber knocked us both down and had made a successful break for liberty. Uncle Peter gave expression to a yell of dismay, and once again he and his bow and arrow held a reunion.

Tacks suggested that we burn the house down so the burglar wouldn't be able to find it if he came around after dark. I thought extremely well of the suggestion, but didn't dare say so.

Aunt Martha had just about decided to untie a fit of hysterics, when Clara J. reached for the kerosene bucket and threw oil on the troubled waters.

"Let's drop all this nonsense about burglars and ghosts and go to breakfast," she suggested. "I don't believe there ever was a ghost within sixty miles of this house, and to save my soul I couldn't be afraid of a burglar whose specialty consisted of falling in the cellar and swearing till help came!"

After breakfast I was dragged away to the brook to fish for lamb chops or whatever kind of an animal it was that Uncle Peter and Tacks decided would bite. Aunt Martha posted off to the city on urgent business, the nature of which she carefully concealed from everybody.

Clara J. said she'd be delighted to have the house all to herself for an hour or two, there were so many rooms to look through and so many plans to make.

Uncle Peter gave her his bow and arrow with full instructions how to shoot if danger threatened, and Tacks carefully rubbed the steps leading up to the piazza with soap so the burglar would fall and break his neck. Then the little shrimp called my attention to his handiwork and demonstrated its availability by slipping thereon himself and going the whole distance on his face. He

26

didn't break his neck, however, so to my mind his burglar alarm failed to make good.

As time wore on I felt more and more like a mock turtle being led to the soup house.

The fact that Bunch was sore worried me, and I began to realize that it was now only a question of a few hours when I'd have to crawl up to Clara J. and hand in my resignation.

Every time I drew a picture of that scene and heard myself telling her I was nothing but a fawn-colored four-flush I could see my future putting on the mitts and getting ready to hand me one.

And when I thought of the dish of fairy tales I had cooked for that girl I could feel something running around in my head and trying to hide. I suppose it was my conscience.

At the brook, Uncle Peter began to throw out hints that he was the original lone fisherman. The lobster never lived that could back away from him, and as for fly-casting, well, he was Piscatorial Peter, the Fancy Fish Charmer from Fishkill.

The old gentleman is very rich, but he loves to live around with his relatives, not because he's stingy, but simply because he likes them and knows they are good listeners.

Uncle Peter is a reformed money-maker. He wrote the first Monopoly that ever made faces at a defenceless public. He was the owner of the first Trust ever captured alive, and he fed it on government bonds and small dealers till it grew tame enough to eat out of a pocketbook.

Uncle Peter sat down on a rock overhanging the clay bank which sloped up about four feet above the lazy brooklet. He carefully arranged his expensive rod, placed his fish basket near by and entered into a dissertation on angling that would make old Ike Walton get up and leave the aquarium.

In the meantime Tacks decided to do some bait fishing, so with an old case knife he sat down behind Uncle Peter and began to dig under the rock for worms.

"Fishing is the sport of kings," the old man chuckled; "an it's a long eel that won't turn when trodden upon. If you're not going to fish, John, do sit down! You're throwing a shadow over the water and that scares the finny monsters. A fish diet is great for the brain, John! You should eat more fish."

"There's many a true word spoken from the chest," I sighed, just as Uncle Peter made his first cast and cleverly wound about eight feet of line around a spruce tree on the opposite bank.

The old man began to boil with excitement as he pulled and tugged in an effort to untangle his line, and just about this time Tacks became the author of another spectacular drama.

In the search for the elusive worm that feverish youth known as Tacks the Human Catastrophe, had finally succeeded in prying the rock loose and immediately thereafter Uncle Peter dropped his rod with a yell of terror and proceeded to follow the man from Cook's.

[Illustration: Tacks—the Boy Disaster.]

The rock reached the brook first, but the old gentleman gave it a warm hustle down the bank and finished a close second. He was in the money, all right.

Tacks also ran—but in an opposite direction.

For some little time my spluttering relative sat dumfounded in about two feet of dirty water, and when finally I dipped him out of the drink he looked like a busy wash-day. Everything was damp hut his ardor.

However, with characteristic good nature he squeezed the water out of his pockets and declared that it was just the kind of exercise he needed. He made me promise not to tell Aunt Martha, because she was very much opposed to his going in bathing on account of the undertow. Then I sneaked him up to his room and left him to change his clothes.

On the piazza I found Clara J., her face shrouded in the after-glow of a wintry sunset.

She handed me a telegram minus the envelope and asked me, with a voice that was intended to be cuttingly sarcastic, "Is there any answer?"

I opened the message and read:

New York.

> John Henry,
> Jiggersville, N. Y.

The two queens will be out this afternoon. They are good girls so treat them white.

Bunch.

The unspeakable idiot, to send me a wire worded like that! No wonder Clara J. was sitting on the ice cream freezer! Of course it only meant that Bunch's sister and her daughter were coming out to look at their property, but— suffering mackerel! what an eye Clara J. was giving me!

"And who are the two queens?" she queried, bitterly.

My face grew redder and redder. Every minute I expected to turn into a complete boiled lobster. I could see somebody reaching for the mayonaise to sprinkle me.

"Well," she continued, "is there no answer? Of course, they are good girls, and you'll treat them white, but—" Then the heavens opened and the floods descended.

"Oh, John!" she sobbed; "how could you be so unkind, so cruel! Think of it, a scandal on the very first day in my new home, and I was so happy!"

I would confess everything. There was no other way out of it. I was on my knees by her side just about to blurt forth the awful truth when my courage failed and suddenly I switched my bet and gave the cards another cut.

"It's all a mistake," I whispered; "it's only Bunch Jefferson doing a comedy scene. Don't you understand, dear; when Bunch tries to get funny all the undertakers have a busy season. I simply don't know who he means by the two queens, and as for scandal, well, you know me, Pete!"

I threw out my chest and gave an imitation of St. Anthony.

"You must know who he means," she insisted, brightening a bit, however.

"Ah, I have it!" I cried, brave-hearted liar that I was; "he means my Aunt Eliza and her daughter, Julia! You remember Aunt Eliza, and Julia?"

"I never heard you speak of them before," she said, still unconvinced.

Good reason, too, for up to this awful moment I never had an Aunt Eliza or a cousin Julia, but relatives must be found to fit the emergency.

"Oh, you've forgotten, my dear," I said, soothingly. "Aunt Eliza and Julia are two of the best Aunts I ever had—er, I mean Aunt Eliza is the best cousin— well, let it go at that! Bunch may have met them on the street, you see, and they inquired for my address. Yes, that's it. Dear, old Aunt Eliza!"

"Is she very old?" Clara J. asked, willing to be convinced if I could deliver the goods.

"Old," I echoed, then suddenly remembering Bunch's description; "oh, no; she's a young widow, about 28 or 41, somewhere along in there. You'll like her immensely, but I hope she doesn't come out until we get settled in a year or two."

Clara J. dried her eyes, but I could see that she hadn't restored me to her confidence as a member in good standing.

She pleaded a headache and went away to her room, while I sat down with Bunch's telegram in my hands and tried to find even a cowpath through the woods.

Uncle Peter came out, none the worse for his cold plunge, and sat down near me.

"Ah, my boy, isn't this delightful!" he cried, drinking in the air. "There's nothing like the country, I tell you! Look at that view! Isn't it grand? John, to be frank with you, up until I saw this place I didn't have much faith in your ability as a business man, but now I certainly admire your wisdom in selecting a spot like this—what did it cost you?"

Cost me! so far it had cost me an attack of nervous prostration, but I couldn't tell him that. I hesitated for the simple reason that I hadn't the faintest idea what the place had cost Bunch. I had been too busy to ask him.

"It's all right, John," the old fellow went on; "don't think me inquisitive. A rubberneck is the root of all evil. It's only because I've been watching you rather closely since we came out here and you seem to be nervous about something. I had an idea maybe it took all your ready money to buy the place, and possibly you regret spending so much—but don't you do it! The best day's work you ever did was when you bought this place!"

"Yes, I believe you!" I sighed, wearily, as I turned to look down the road.

I stiffened in the chair for I saw my finish in the outward form of two women rapidly approaching the house,

"It's Bunch's sister and her daughter," I moaned to myself. "Well, I'll be generous and let the blow fall first on Uncle Peter!" Accordingly, I made a quick exit,

In the kitchen I found Clara J., her headache forgotten, busily preparing to cook the dinner.

She's a foxy little bundle of peaches, that girl is; and I was wise to the fact that her suspicion factory was still working over-time, turning out material for the undersigned.

I felt it in my bones that the steer I gave her about Aunt Eliza had been placed in cold storage for safe keeping.

Her brain was busy running to the depot to meet the scandal Bunch's telegram hinted at, but she pretended to catch step and walk along with me.

"John," she said, "I certainly do hope your relatives won't come out for some little time, because we really aren't ready for visitors, now are we, dear?"

"Indeed we are not," I groaned.

"I can't help thinking it awfully strange that you should be notified of their coming by Mr. Jefferson, and in such peculiar language," she said, after a pause.

"Didn't I tell you Bunch is a low comedian," I said, weakly.
"Besides, he knows them very well. Aunt Fanny is very fond of Bunch."

"Aunt Fanny," she repeated, dropping a tin pan to the floor with a crash; "I thought you said her name was Eliza?"

"Sure thing!" I chortled; while my heart fell off its perch and dropped in my shoes. "Her name is Eliza Fanny; some of us call her Aunt Eliza, some Aunt Fanny—see?"

She hadn't time to see, for at that moment Tacks rushed in, exclaiming, "Say, sister, they's two strange women on the piazza talking to Uncle Peter, and maybe when they go one of them will fall down the steps if I put some more soap there!"

Like a whirlwind he was gone again. Clara J. simply looked at me queerly and said, "The queens are here; treat them white, John!"

I felt as happy as a piece of cheese.

CHAPTER VI.

"Well!" said Clara J., after a painful pause, "why don't you go and welcome your Aunt Eliza?"

Aunt Lize would be the central figure in a hot old time if she went where I wished her at that moment.

Somebody had tied both my feet to the floor.

I had visions of two excited females lambasting me with umbrellas and demanding their property back.

Completely at a loss I sank into a chair, feeling as bright and chipper as a poached egg.

I felt that I belonged just about as much as a knothole does in a barb-wire fence.

In that few minutes Bunch was more than revenged.

I was on the pickle boat for sure.

Sailing! sailing! over the griddle, me!

Scientists tell us that when a man is drowning every detail of his lifetime passes before him in the fraction of a second.

Well, that moving picture gag was worked on me, without the aid of a bathing suit.

When I awoke, Clara J. was saying, "Possibly it would look better if I went with you. Wait just a moment, till I get this apron off—there! come along!"

I arose, and with delightful unanimity the chair arose also, clinging like a passionate porusplaster to my pantaloons.

"Mercy'" exclaimed Clara J., "that little villain, Tacks, has been making molasses candy!"

"It strikes me," I said, trying hard to be calm, "that after making the candy he decided to make a monkey of me. Darn the blame thing, it won't let go! I suppose I've got to be a perpetual furniture mover the rest of my life!"

Just then Uncle Peter came bubbling into the kitchen, talking in short explosions like a bottle of vichy, and I collaborated with the chair in a hasty squatty-vous!

"Two women on the piazza," he fizzed; "been talking to them an hour and all I could get out of them was 'yes' and 'no.' Not bad looking, but profoundly dumb."

"Hush!" said Clara J., glancing uneasily at me and then back at Uncle Peter, as she raised a warning finger to her lips.

"Oh, they can't hear me," the old gentleman went on; "John, you better go out and see them. They have a card with your name written on it. I'm no lady's man, anyhow."

"Do they look like queens?" Clara J. asked, uneasily.

"Well, they aren't exactly Cleopatras, but not bad, not bad!" he gurgled.

"Is one older than the other?" Clara J. cross-questioned.

"Might be mother and daughter," Uncle Peter fancied.

"It's surely Bunch's bunch," I groaned inwardly, wondering how I'd look galloping across the country with a kitchen chair trailing along behind.

"Uncle Peter, it must be John Henry's Aunt Eliza and cousin Julia. He expects them, don't you, John?" Clara J. explained. "We shall be ready to welcome them in just a little while;" here she glanced cautiously at the chair. "In the meantime you show them into the spare room and say that John will see them very soon."

The old gentleman eyed me suspiciously and retired without a word.

I'm afraid Uncle Peter found it hard to take.

With the kind assistance of the carving knife Clara J. removed all of me from the chair, with the exception of a few feet of trousers, and I made a quick change of costume.

A few minutes later I joined her in the parlor, where the scene was set for my finish. I picked out a quiet spot near the piano to die.

Uncle Peter was enjoying every minute of it.

He hurried off to escort the visitors to the parlor and a moment later Aunt Martha bustled in.

"Are they here?" she asked breathlessly.

"How did you know they were coming?" inquired Clara J. in surprised tones.

"How did I know!" exclaimed Auntie; "why I sent them!"

Every hand was against me. The parachute had failed to work and I was dropping on the rocks.

Faintly and far away I could hear the ambulance coming at a gallop.

Sweet spirits of ammonia, but I was up against it!

It was plainly evident to me that Aunt Martha knew the awful relatives of Bunch, and that the old lady was camping on my trial. Yes; there she stood, old Aunt Nemesis, glaring at me from behind her spectacles.

I decided to die without going over near the piano.

"Where are they?" I could hear Aunt Martha asking in the same tone of voice I was certain the Roman Emperor used when just about to frame up a finale for a few Christians from over the Tiber.

"Uncle Peter has gone for them; we put them in the spare room," answered Clara J.

"What! *in the spare room!*" gasped Aunt Martha, collapsing in a chair just as Uncle Peter appeared in the doorway, bowing low before the visitors, who stalked clumsily into the parlor.

For some reason or other Clara J. omitted the formality of springing forward and greeting my relatives effusively, so she simply said, "You are very welcome, Aunt Eliza and cousin Julia!"

"Great heavens! what does this mean?" shrieked Aunt Martha. "It cannot be possible that these two women are relatives of yours, John! Why, I engaged them both in an intelligence office; one for the kitchen, the other as parlor maid!"

"Sure not," I chirped, in joy-freighted accents, as I grasped the glorious situation. "They aren't my relatives and never were. The more I look at them the more convinced I am that there's no room for them to perch on my family tree. I disown them both. Back to the woods with the Swede imposters!"

I win by an eyelash.

I was so happy I went over to the mantel and began to bite the bric-a-brac.

Clara J. didn't know whether to laugh or cry, so she compromised by giggling at Uncle Peter, who sat on the piano stool whirling himself around rapidly and muttering, "any kind of exercise is good exercise."

Aunt Martha stared around the room from one to another in speechless amazement, while the two innocent causes of all the trouble stood motionless, with their noses tip-tilted to the ceiling.

Presently Aunt Martha broke the spell just as I was about to eat a cut-glass vase in the gladness of my heart.

"Go to the kitchen!" she said sharply to the newcomers, whereupon they both turned in unison and looked the old lady all over. Finally they decided to discharge Aunt Martha, for the oldest member of the troupe folded her arms decisively and said, "Sure, it ain't in any lunatic asylum I'll be afther livin', bless th' Saints! If yez have a sinsible moment left in your head will yez give us th' car fare back to th' city, and it'll be a blessed hour for me whin I plants me feet on th' ferryboat, so it will!"

Uncle Peter checked the fiery course of the piano stool and began to make his double chin do a gurgle, whereupon the youngest of the two female impersonators handed him a glare that put out his chuckle and he started the piano stool again at the rate of 45 revolutions per minute.

"Th' ould buffalo over there showed us up to th' spare room, thinkin' to be funny," she who was fated never to be our cook, went on, "and if I wasn't in a daffy house and him nothin' but a bug it's the weight of that chair he'd feel over his bald spot. Th' ould goosehead, to set us down on th' porch and talk to us for an hour about th' landshcape and th' atmusphere, and to ask me, a respectable lady, what kind of exercise I was partial to! It's a Hiven's own blessin' I didn't hand him a poke in th' slats, so it is!"

Uncle Peter, with palpably assumed indifference, slid off the piano stool and faded behind the furthermost window curtain, while I went up to the belligerent visitor and said, "On your way, Gismonda; the referee gives the fight to you; here's the gate receipts!"

With this I handed her a ten-spot which she looked at suspiciously and said, "If ever I get that ould potato pounder over in New York it's exercise I'll give him! Sure, I'll run him from th' Bat'hry to Harlem widout a shtop for meals, bad cess to him!"

Having delivered this parting knock at Uncle Peter, the queen of the kitchen flounced out of the house, followed by the younger one who had played only a thinking part in the strenuous scene.

Aunt Martha still sat motionless in the chair, quite on the verge of tears, when Clara J. went over to her and said, "Why didn't you tell me you were going after servants, Auntie?"

"I wanted to surprise you," the old lady replied, plaintively.
"They were to be my contribution to the household."

"You handed us a surprise, all right; didn't she, Uncle Peter?" I chirped in with a view to laughing off the whole affair, but just then a series of startling shrieks caused us all to rush for the piazza.

At the gate we beheld a kicking, struggling mass of lingerie and bad dialect, which presently resolved itself into the forms of my temporary relatives who were now busily engaged in macadamizing the roadway with their heads.

Then Tacks came yelling on the scene: "I thought maybe they was female burglars so I stretched a wire acrost the gate and they was in such a hurry getting away that they never noticed it till it was too everlastingly late!"

Before we could remonstrate with the Boy-Disaster he let another whoop out of him and darted off in the direction of the barn.

That whoop brought the two wire-tappers to their feet and after they both shook their fists eagerly in our direction they started in frenzied haste for the depot.

As they scurried frantically out of our neighborhood Uncle Peter smiled blandly and murmured, "For lecturers, female reformers and all those who lead a sedentary life there's nothing like exercise!"

Putting my arm around Clara J.'s waist I whispered, "Didn't I tell you it was one of Bunch's put-up jobs? He's jealous because I'm so happy out here with you, that's all! As for the telegram, forget it!"

"All right, John," said Clara J., "but nevertheless that same telegram gave you a busy day, didn't it?"

"It surely did, but it was only because I hated to have you worried," I answered as she went in the house to console Aunt Martha.

I sat down in a chair expecting every moment to have the Prince of Liars come up and congratulate me.

Humming a tune quietly to himself Uncle Peter watched the flying squadron disappear in a bend of the road, then he sat down near me and said, "John, you're worried about something and I've a pretty fair idea what it is. This property is too big a load for you to carry, eh?"

From the depths of my heart I replied, "It certainly is!"

"Well," said the old gentleman, "it surely has made a hit with me. I never struck a place I liked half as well as this. How would you like to sell it to me, then you and Clara J. could live with us, eh? Come on, now, what d'ye say?"

I sat there utterly unable to say anything.

"What did it cost you; come on, now, John?" the old fellow urged.

"Oh, about $14,000," I whispered, picking out the first figure I could think of.

"It's worth it and more, too," he said. "I'll give you $20,000 for it—say the word!"

"Well, if you insist!" I replied, weakly; and the next minute he danced off to write me a check.

In the tar barrel every time I opened my mouth! Hard luck was certainly putting the wrapping paper all over me.

Well, the only thing to do now was to hustle up to town in the morning and inform Bunch that I had sold his property.

I felt sure he'd be tickled to a stand-still—not!

CHAPTER VII.

JOHN HENRYS HAPPY HOME.

Early the next morning I broke camp and took the trail to town, determined never to come back alive unless Bunch agreed to sell the plantation to Uncle Peter.

The old gentleman had crowded his check for $20,000 into my trembling hands the night before with instructions to deposit it in my bank, and at my convenience I was to let him have the deed to the place.

Well, if Bunch should refuse to play ball I could send the check back to Uncle Peter, and a telegram to Clara J., telling her that I was back in the flat, laid up with a spavined fetlock or something.

Uncle Peter was out in the garden planting puree of split peas or some other spring vegetable when I started for the train, so all the Recording Angel had to put down against me was the new batch of Ochiltrees I told Clara J.

I soon located Bunch, and to my surprise found him more inclined to josh than to jolt.

[Illustration: Bunch Jefferson—All to the Good and Two to Carry.]

"Ah! my friend from the bush!" he exclaimed; "are you in town to buy imitation coal, or is it to get a derrick and hoist your home affairs away from my property? Why don't you take a tumble, John, and let go?"

"Bunch," I said, "believe me, this is the crudest game of freeze-out I ever sat in. My throat is sore from singing, 'Father, dear father, come home with me now!' and every move I make nets me a new ornamentation on my neck. Why didn't I tell the good wife that the ponies put the crimp in my pocketbook instead of crawling into this chasm of prevarication and trouble?"

"You can search me!" Bunch answered, thoughtfully.

"And that phony wire you sent me yesterday almost gave me a plexus," I said bitterly. "Why did you frame up one of those when-we-were-twenty-one dispatches from the front? It sounded like a love song from Willie Hayface of Cohoes, after his first day on Broadway. Didn't you know that my wife was liable to open that queer fellow and put me on the toasting fork?"

Bunch blinked his eyes solemnly, but when I told him all about the trouble his telegram had caused he simply rose up on his hind legs and laughed me to a sit down.

"Well," he gasped after a long fit of cackling; "sister did intend going out to Jiggersville and the only way I could stop her was to suddenly discover that her health wasn't any too good, so I chased her off to Virginia Hot Springs for a couple of weeks."

After all, Bunch had his redeeming qualities.

"I sent you that wire before I took sister's temperature," Bunch explained, "and I quite forgot to send another which would put a copper on the queens."

Once more he laughed uproariously and chortled between the outbursts, "Now—ha, ha, ha!—I'm even for—ha, ha, ha!—for that shoot the chute I did in your—ha, ha, ha—in your cellar—oh! ha, ha, ha, ha!"

"Oh, quit your kidding!" I begged, and then, suddenly, "Say, Bunch, will you sell the old homestead?"

Bunch stopped laughing and looked me over from head to foot. "Is this on the level or simply another low tackle?"

"It's the goods," I answered: "I simply can't frighten, coax, scare, drive or push my home companions away from your property, so I'd like to buy it if you're game to cut the cards?"

"Been playing the lottery?" he snickered.

"No, but I have the Pierponts, all right, all right," I replied; "will you put $14,000 in your kick and pass me over the baronial estate?"

"Fourteen thousand!" Bunch repeated slowly. "Sure, I will. If you can Morgan that amount I'll make good with the necessary documents, and then you and your family troubles may sit around on fly paper in Jiggersville for the rest of your natural lives for all I care."

I explained to Bunch that I wanted the deed made out in the name of Peter Grant for the reason that Uncle Peter was a bigger farmer than I, and in short order the preliminary arrangements were completed to the satisfaction and relief of both parties concerned.

That evening I went back to Jiggersville feeling as light as a pin feather on a young duck.

Uncle Peter could have the property; Bunch could buy his sister another castle, and I was ahead of the game just $6,000, more than enough to square me for all the green paper I had torn up at the track.

Of course, it did look as though Uncle Peter had been whipsawed, but when I considered the bundles the old gentleman had stored away in the vaults, and when I remembered his eagerness to cough, I simply couldn't produce one pang of conscience.

Two days later Bunch had a certified check for $14,000 and Uncle Peter was the happy owner of the country estate.

"We will live with you and Aunt Martha a little while," I said to him; "but if you have no objection I'd like to buy a small lot down near the brook from you and build a bit of a cage there for ourselves."

Uncle Peter chuckled affirmatively, but seemed unwilling to continue the subject further. "Isn't it glorious out here," he smiled. "Pure air, fresh from the bakery of Heaven! I have younged myself ten years since we came out here. Yesterday I fell in a bear trap which Tacks had dug and carefully concealed with brush and leaves. It took me four hours to get out because I'm rather stout, but the exercise surely did me good."

Can you beat him?

A week later the second anniversary of our wedding would roll around, and although Clara J. was a trifle hard to win over, I finally coaxed her to let me have Bunch out to spend a few hours with us on that occasion.

At the appointed hour Bunch arrived and Clara J. greeted him with every word of that telegram darting forth darkly from her eyes.

"Mrs. John," said Bunch, "I'm simply delighted to know you. I've often heard your husband speak well of you."

She had to smile in spite of herself.

"Mrs. John," Bunch went on, with splendid assurance; "you should be proud of this matinee idol husband of yours, for, to tell you the truth, he's all the goods—he certainly is."

Clara J. looked somewhat embarrassed, and as for me, I was away out to sea in an open boat. I hadn't the faintest idea what Bunch was driving at.

"You surely have a wonderful influence over him," the lad with the blarney continued. "A week or so ago I threw some bait at him just to test him and he didn't even nibble. You know, in the old days John and I often trotted in double harness to the track—bad place for young men—sure!"

Bunch surveyed the property with a quick glance and said, "Yes, I sent John a telegram. 'The two queens will be out this afternoon,' I wired, meaning two horses that simply couldn't lose. 'They are good girls, so treat them white,' I told him, meaning that he should put up his roll on them and win a hatfull; but, Mrs. John, I never touched him. He simply ignored my telegram and sat around in the hammock all day, reading a novel, I suppose. I apologize to you, Mrs. John, for trying to drag him away from the path of rectitude, but, believe me, I didn't know when I sent the message that he had promised you to give the ponies the long farewell!"

Clara J. laughed with happiness, all her doubts dispersed, and said, "Oh, don't mention it, Mr. Bunch! I'm simply delighted to welcome you to our new home. You have never been out here before, have you?"

Bunch glanced at me, then through the open front door in the direction of the scene of his downfall, and said, hesitatingly, "Never before, thank you, kindly!"

Good old Bunch. He had squared me with my wife and the world—oh, well, some day, perhaps, I'd get a chance to even up.

"John," he said, a few minutes later, when we took a short stroll around the place. "Now that I've started in to tell the whole truth I musn't skip a paragraph. This is a pleasant bit of property, but the solemn fact remains that I put the boots to you. I gave you the gaff for $6,000, old friend, and it breaks my heart to tell you that I'm not sorry. Bunch for Number One, always!"

"What do you mean?" I asked.

"This farm only cost me $8,000," he said, giving me the pitying grin.

"It cost me $14,000 and I sold it for $20,000," I said, slowly.

We stopped and shook hands.

"Who's the come-on?" he asked, presently.

"Uncle Peter," I answered, "but the old boy has so much he has to kick a lot of it out of the house every once in a while, so it's all right."

After dinner we were all sitting on the piazza listening to a treatise from Uncle Peter on the subject of the growth and proper care of wheat cakes, or asparagus, I forget which, when suddenly the cadaverous form of the Sherlock Holmes of Jiggersville appeared before us.

"Evenin' all!" bowed Harmony Diggs, clinging tightly to a bundle which he held under his arm.

"Find that robber yet?" inquired Bunch, winking at me.

"That's just what I dropped around for to tell you, thinkin' maybe you'd be kinder interested in knowin' the facts in the case," Harmony went on, carefully placing the precious bundle on the steps.

"I got a clue from this here gent," he said, pointing a bony finger at Bunch, "and I ups and chases that there maleyfactor for four miles, well knowin' that the cause of justice would suffer and the reward of fifty dollars be nil and voidless if the critter got away. But I got him, by crickey, I got him!"

He looked from one to the other, seeking a sign of applause, and Bunch said, "Where did you catch him?"

"About four miles yonder," Diggs explained, indefinitely. "It was a fierce fight while it lasted, but they ain't no maleyfactor livin' can escape the clutches of these here hands oncet they entwines him. I pulled the dem cuss out of his clothes!"

With this thrilling announcement he opened the bundle and proudly displayed the burglar harness which Bunch had worn on that memorable night.

"And the burglar himself?" Bunch questioned.

Diggs raised his head slowly, and with theatrical effect answered, "I give the cussed scoun'rel the doggonest drubbin' a mortal maleyfactor ever got and let him go. That was nearly two weeks ago, and he ain't showed up since, dag him!"

"You win, Mr. Ananias!" said Bunch, handing Diggs a ten dollar bill, as he whispered to me, "That story is worth the money."

"What's that for?" inquired Diggs, somewhat taken aback.

"That's my contribution to the reward for the robber," Bunch told him.

"Well," spluttered Diggs; "it don't seem zactly right, seein' as how I on'y pulled the cuss out of his clothes and then let him go with a lambastin'."

"The ten-spot is for the clothes you pulled him out of," Bunch said, picking up the garments and handing them to me. "Keep them, John, as a souvenir of your first burglar—and true friend, Bunch!"

I took them reverently, and said, "For your sake, Bunch, they'll be handed down from generation to generation."

Clara J. blushed and said, "Oh, John!" and I thought Uncle Peter would chuckle himself into a delirium.

"Good-night, Mr. Ananias!" Bunch called, as Diggs made a farewell bow and turned to go.

"Good-night, one and all," replied Diggs, then a thought struck him and he turned with, "Say, who's this here Mr. Annienias? Seems like the name's familiar, but it ain't mine."

"Mr. Ananias is the first detective mentioned in history," Bunch explained, and Mr. Diggs beamed over us all.

"Wait a moment, Mr. Officer," Aunt Martha piped in; "have a drop of refreshment before you go. Tacks, run in and pour Mr. Officer a drink from that bottle on the sideboard!"

Diggs stood there swallowing his palate in delightful anticipation until Tacks handed him a brimming glass from which the brave thief-taker took one eager mouthful, whereupon he emitted a shriek of terror that could be heard for miles.

"Water! water! quick! I'm a'burnin' up!" cried the astonished Diggs.

Uncle Peter in his eagerness to quench the flames poured half a pitcher full of ice water down the back of Diggs' neck.

"It ain't there, it's down my throat!" yelled the unfortunate Harmony, whereupon Uncle Peter poured the rest of the ice water over the constable's head.

When, finally, the old fellow was revived he faintly declined any more refreshment, and with a sad "good-night," faded away in the twilight.

"Gee!" exclaimed Tacks, as he watched the retreating form, "I'm afraid I upset some tobascum sauce in that glass by mistake."

Presently, Bunch went off to the depot to take a train back to the city, and for some little time we sat in silence on the piazza.

"Grand, isn't it?" Uncle Peter said, breaking the spell. "Couldn't be any nicer, now, could it?" Then he went over and stood near Clara J.

"Little woman," he said; "ever since we first talked of moving out here I noticed how worried John was."

"So did I," she answered, taking my hand in hers.

"A day or two ago I found out what the trouble was," the old gentleman continued; "this property was too heavy a load for a young man to carry, especially when he's just married, so I bought it from him!"

Before Clara J. could express a word Uncle Peter put his arm around Aunt Martha's waist and continued, "Aunt Martha and I talked it all over last night and in celebration of your second anniversary we want you to accept this little present," and with this he placed a document in Clara J.'s hands.

"It's the deed to the property," Aunt Martha said, "all for you, Clara J., but if you don't mind, we'd like to live here!"

"Yes," said Uncle Peter; "that garden certainly needs someone to look after it!"

Clara J. was crying softly and hugging Aunt Martha,

My own eyes were damp and I yearned to have somebody run the lawn mower over me.

"I'll race you down to the gate and back," I suggested.

"You're on," laughed Uncle Peter; "I believe I do need a little exercise!"

Lightning Source UK Ltd.
Milton Keynes UK
UKHW012018130123
415332UK00003B/100

9 783752 360899